P9-COO-533

RUDOLPH
· THE · RED · NOSED ·
REINDEER®

Adapted from the story by Robert L. May

Retold by Robin Cohen
Illustrated by Phil Ortiz and Robbin Cuddy

A GOLDEN BOOK · NEW YORK

Western Publishing Company, Inc., Racine, Wisconsin 53404

© 1993 Robert L. May Company. All rights reserved. Published by arrangement with Modern Curriculum Press, Inc. Printed in the U.S.A. No part of this book may be reproduced or copied in any form without written permission from the copyright owner. All other trademarks are the property of Western Publishing Company, Inc.
Library of Congress Catalog Card Number: 92-75177 ISBN: 0-307-30114-1   MCMXCIV

Once upon a time, in a land far to the north, lived a good little reindeer named Rudolph. He was younger than most of the other reindeer, and there was something else about him that was different, too. His nose was bright red. You could even say it glowed.

The other reindeer played together all day and
had fun. But they never let Rudolph join in
their games. They laughed at him and called
him names—like Rudolph the Red-Nosed
Reindeer.

Rudolph did not like being teased. He often
felt sad and lonely.

When Christmas Eve came, Rudolph felt
happy at last. Santa would soon be coming with
gifts for everyone, even for a little reindeer with
a bright red nose.

Rudolph made sure everything was ready for
Santa's visit. His stocking was hung. A snack
was waiting for Santa.

"Sweet dreams, my good little reindeer," said Rudolph's mother as she tucked him into bed. The little reindeer went to sleep feeling hopeful and excited. Santa was coming!

As animals and children around the world fell
asleep, Santa and his elves were at the North
Pole packing the sleigh for the night's journey.

While they worked, a terrible fog rolled in.
Santa began to worry about the bad weather.

"This fog! What a bother!" he complained. "It
will surely slow us down!"

Soon all was ready. The toys and gifts were
loaded, the reindeer were all harnessed, and
Santa was at the reins.

"Come Dasher! Come Dancer!
Come Prancer and Vixen!
Come Comet! Come Cupid!
Come Donner and Blitzen!"

Santa called to the reindeer, and up they rose into the dark night sky—without a single star to light their way.

Santa guided the reindeer carefully through the misty sky. But flying was slow and difficult.

"Whoa there!" Santa called finally, pulling on the reins. As they came down for a landing, the sleigh grazed the tops of several small trees.

"Dash it all!" said Santa. "It's too foggy to see my way clear!"

By the time Santa arrived at Rudolph's house, he was way behind schedule and worried indeed. How would he deliver all the rest of the gifts?

When Santa opened the door to Rudolph's room, he saw a bright red glow. Then he saw that the light was coming from Rudolph's nose. A wonderful idea popped into his head!

Santa woke the little reindeer gently.
"Rudolph, you're a dream come true!" said
Santa. "Your light is the answer! Won't you
come and guide my sleigh tonight?"
Rudolph sat up in his bed. He could not
believe his ears. Santa was asking for his help!

Rudolph climbed out of bed quickly. He left a note for his parents, telling them not to worry and that he had gone to lead Santa's sleigh.

Then Rudolph ran outside with Santa. The other reindeer were waiting impatiently. Santa quickly fixed a harness for Rudolph at the head of the team.

"Ho! Ho! Ho!" Santa chuckled. "Come along, Rudolph! Come lead us with your light through this dreadfully foggy night!"

With Rudolph in the lead, they took off into the dark night once more.

It was a wonderful journey. In spite of the fog, they flew quickly and low. With Rudolph's bright nose to steer by, the reindeer didn't hit a single treetop. And Santa made up for the lost time, delivering all the presents for all the children around the world.

As the sun came up on Christmas morning, Rudolph's parents were waiting for him to come home. With great pride they told all of the other reindeer that their son, Rudolph, had guided Santa's sleigh through the foggy night.

A crowd watched the sky. The reindeer wanted to see for themselves if the rumor was true.

"There they are!" shouted one reindeer. "It is true!" shouted another. "Rudolph really is leading the sleigh!"

After the sleigh landed, the reindeer all cheered for Rudolph.

Santa thanked his number-one reindeer in front of the crowd. "Without you, Rudolph, we would have been lost," he said. "Will you lead us again on the next foggy Christmas Eve?"

Rudolph agreed, feeling very proud—and very happy. And from that time on, Rudolph the Red-Nosed Reindeer was the most famous reindeer of all.